This Little Tiger book belongs to:

_____

_____

_____

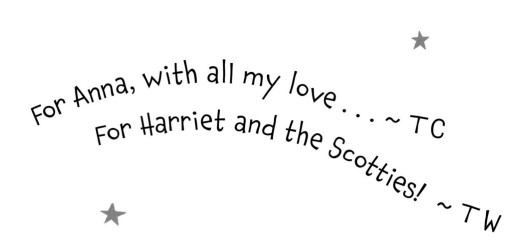

For Anna, with all my love . . . ~ TC
For Harriet and the Scotties! ~ TW

LITTLE TIGER PRESS LTD,
an imprint of the Little Tiger Group
1 Coda Studios, 189 Munster Road, London SW6 6AW
www.littletiger.co.uk

First published in Great Britain 2012
This edition published 2018

A CIP catalogue record for this book is available from the British Library

All rights reserved • ISBN 978-1-78881-193-4

Printed in China
LTP/2700/2550/1018
2 4 6 8 10 9 7 5 3

"Wheeeeeeeeee!"

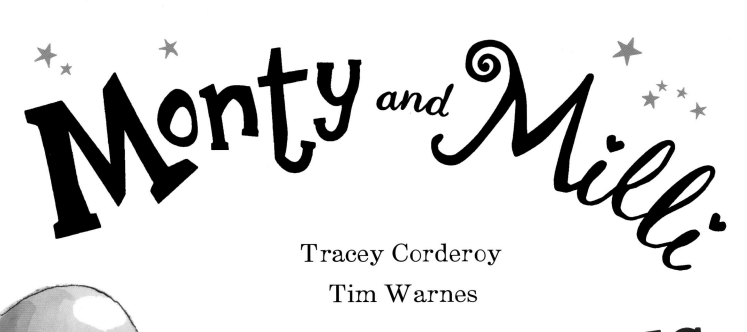

Monty and Milli

Tracey Corderoy

Tim Warnes

The Totally AMAZING Magic Trick

LITTLE TIGER

LONDON

Everything Monty did...

Milli did too.

CRASH!

When Monty roared, Milli roared.

When Monty painted...
so did Milli!

And, whenever Monty curled up with his favourite book…

Read to me, Monty – pleeeease?

guess who always showed up with **hers**?!

"No Milli," he said,
"it's meant for **one**..."

one hat.

She took it rather
well, considering.

"Kazoom!"

But it was
no good – Croaky just
wouldn't disappear.

Ribbit!

"Actually," piped up Milli, "magicians always shut their eyes."

Monty shut his eyes. "**Kazaam**?" he said. He peeped through his fingers...

...he'd done it!

"Whoopee!" yelled Monty.
"I'm **magic!**"

Hee hee!

But **something** just didn't feel **quite** right...

"Milli!"

cried Monty.

His sister sniffed. "I only wanted to help."
"Well, **don't!**" Monty scowled.

But then Monty remembered –
all the best tricks had helpers…
"Ok," he said. "You can help.
But no taking over."
"**Me**?" squeaked Milli.
"But I **never**
take over…

…*EVER!*"

Milli **tried** not taking over.

Watch this, Monty...

She tried again and again until...

"Whoops!"

RRRRIPPP!

For the rest of the day Monty practised his magic **without** Milli's help. He practised on his tadpole.
(Who didn't complain.)

Pick a card – any card...

Then he practised on his granny.
(Who did.)

Rope tricks
1
2
3

Sometimes things went a little bit wrong but Monty didn't care!

Being by himself, for once, was fun!

"Monty…" said Dad at teatime, "where's Milli? Have you seen her?"

Monty checked behind his back. Then around his legs. Milli wasn't in any of her **usual** places. "Nope," he shrugged. "No Milli."

Then he gasped.
"Oh no! I think I've turned my sister into
a **warty toad**!"

Monty sniffed. "I didn't **mean** it!
I love her really."

"Surprise!"
squealed Milli, shooting out
from under the table.

She gave her Monty a **huge** Milli hug.
"You didn't magic me really, **silly**!" she giggled.

Later, when Monty snuggled up,
Milli snuggled up too. "Monty," she said sleepily,
"you **are** magic, I'm sure."

"Really?" grinned Monty.
"**Very** really," Milli
grinned back.

She closed her eyes and he closed his.

"Think of a **huge**, fluffy bunny…" she yawned,

"and I bet you'll magic it up!"

"I wish…" smiled Monty, drifting off to sleep.

Totally Amazing Magic Tricks

The wand slipped from his fingers and…

FWIP!